Shh!
Don't Wake the Baby!

For Thea and John

Published by Bonney Press,
an imprint of Hinkler Books Pty Ltd
45–55 Fairchild Street
Heatherton Victoria 3202 Australia
www.hinkler.com.au

BONNEY
PRESS

Originally published by Fernleigh Books, London

© Cat's Pyjamas 2012, 2014
Text © Cat's Pyjamas 2009
Illustrations © Petra Brown 2009

Prepress: Graphic Print Group

ISBN: 978 1 7436 3505 6

Printed and bound in China

Shh!
Don't Wake the Baby!

Petra Brown

BONNEY
PRESS

In amongst the shady trees, and close by the waterhole, Mama Elephant had just got her new baby off to sleep.

"Now, Little Elephant," she said to her son, "Please be very quiet this afternoon, so that you don't wake the baby."

Little Elephant loved his mama, and wanted to be good.

"OK, Mama. I'll be quiet!" he said, and he gave her a big kiss, and ran off to find something quiet to do.

Little Elephant wasn't known
for being quiet. He could make
a big hullabaloo doing even the
smallest thing! So he crashed through
the forest, trampled down the
undergrowth, and generally
made an awful, joyful din.

Giraffe stretched down
her long neck and said,
"Shh! Don't wake the baby!"

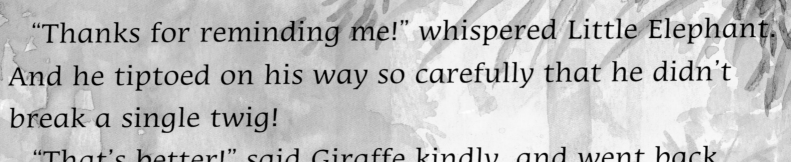

"Thanks for reminding me!" whispered Little Elephant. And he tiptoed on his way so carefully that he didn't break a single twig!

"That's better!" said Giraffe kindly, and went back to her lunch. The forest was quiet once more.

Of all his most fun things to do, bathing in the waterhole was Little Elephant's best. So at the water's edge, he didn't stop to think, he just dived in with a huge...

SPLASH!

Then he noisily sucked up a trunkful of cool muddy water, and poured it over his head. What bliss!

But Hippo, amongst others,
was not impressed.
"Shh! Don't wake the baby!" she glared at him.

"Whoops!" said Little Elephant. "I need to find a quieter way of getting clean!" Gingerly he climbed out of the water, and had a quiet shower instead of a noisy bath.

Once he was clean, Little Elephant was ravenous! So he rushed to the most delicious tree, and took a huge trunkful of sweet juicy leaves.

"Yum!" he slurped, and pulled down another branch, making the whole tree shake and shudder. He had no idea that he was making a big noise, but he was! Grandpa Vervet scowled and hissed at him,

"Ssh! You'll wake that baby, you know!"

"I'm just eating like everyone else!"
pleaded Little Elephant.

"But you're bigger and messier and noisier
than everyone else," said the monkey crossly.
Then, seeing that Little Elephant was truly
upset, he and the other monkeys showed
him how to eat more quietly.

Little Elephant was miserable. He couldn't do any of his most fun things without being noisy. And he'd never had so many tellings off in one day!

He gave a big sigh,
and settled down
to consider how
unfair it all was.

All of a sudden, he got a
funny feeling in his trunk.
It was a bit like a tickle...
or was it more of a
snuffle? Little Elephant
blinked and shook his
tickly trunk from side
to side.

"Something's going to happen," he thought, "and it isn't going to be quiet!" He gave a gasping, helpless snort and...

ATCHOO!!!

"YOU'VE WOKEN THE BABY!!"
groaned Mama Elephant.

Flowers and leaves fluttered down around them. One flower landed in Baby's cradle. All the animals held their breath, waiting for her to scream...

...but Baby just giggled!
"Phew!" said Little Elephant.